D0099490

Given by
Friends of the
Saratoga Libraries
in honor of
Anne-Marie Steele
for volunteer work in the
Marshall Lane School Library
SANTA CLARA COUNTY LIBRARY

THE TERRIBLE TROLL-BIRD

Other books by Ingri and Edgar Parin d'Aulaire

D'Aulaires' Book of Animals
D'Aulaires' Book of Norse Myths
D'Aulaires' Book of Trolls
The Two Cars

Ingri and Edgar Parin d'Aulaire

The Terrible Troll-Bird

THE NEW YORK REVIEW CHILDREN'S COLLECTION
New York

THIS IS A NEW YORK REVIEW BOOK

PUBLISHED BY THE NEW YORK REVIEW OF BOOKS

1755 Broadway, New York, NY 10019

www.nyrb.com

Published in the United States of America

Library of Congress Cataloging-in-Publication Data

D'Aulaire, Ingri, 1904-1980.

The terrible troll-bird / by Ingri and Edgar Parin d'Aulaire.

p. cm. — (New York Review children's collection)

Summary: When four children defeat the terrible troll-bird who has terrified their Norwegian valley for years, everyone celebrates in a merry feast.

ISBN-13: 978-1-59017-252-0 (alk. paper)

ISBN-10: 1-59017-252-3 (alk. paper)

[1. Trolls—Fiction. 2. Norway—Fiction. 3. Fairy tales.] I. D'Aulaire, Edgar Parin, 1898-1986. II. Title.

PZ8.A9238Te 2007

[E]—dc22

2007013020

ISBN 978-1-59017-252-0

Cover design by Louise Fili Ltd.

This book is printed on acid-free paper.

Manufactured in China by P. Chan & Edward, Inc.

1 3 5 7 9 10 8 6 4 2

For
Nils Peter

This is a story
about what happened to
Ola and his sisters, Lina, Sina, and Trina,
who lived in a faraway valley
among the mountains
of Norway.

On a clear summer eve their mother said to them, "Now go up to the grove and fetch me a load of wood for the stove." So off they set. It was lovely in the forest twilight and Ola, Lina, Sina, and Trina ran and jumped and played. Blakken, their good old horse, trotted behind with the cart.

Suddenly they stopped and stood as though fixed to the ground.

For high up in a tree they saw a huge bird that looked at them with evil eyes.

The bird opened its great beak and crowed, and the squawk was so loud that all the trees in the forest trembled and shook.

"Did you hear what the bird crowed?" asked Ola.

"Yes, yes, yes," cried Lina, Sina, and Trina. "It wants to fly off with our Blakken."

And away they ran and stumbled and fell . . .

right home to the farm in the valley. Now Blakken was the first.

Their mother was busy feeding the pigs. She looked in surprise at the empty cart. "Where is the wood you were to bring?" she asked.

"We can't bring any wood today," said Ola, "for a big, bad bird wants to take our Blakken."

"I have never heard such silly talk, to think that a bird could fly off with a horse," said their mother.

But as she turned around she saw the huge bird landing on top of the storehouses. It was so big it had to perch on both roofs.

"Oh, for all the world's pancakes," she cried. "It is the terrible rooster that belongs to the trolls in the mountain."

And the terrible troll-bird it was! It sometimes flew out of the mountain at dusk looking for animals to carry off. Now it had set its eyes on fat, old Blakken.

"Don't be afraid," said Ola to Blakken. "We'll save you." He ran into the house. There on the wall hung an old blunderbuss. He pulled a silver button off his coat and put it into the blunderbuss. For a button of real silver is the only thing sure to hit a troll-bird.

Just then the bird crowed again and flapped its giant wings. The storehouses tottered and everything loose flew about.

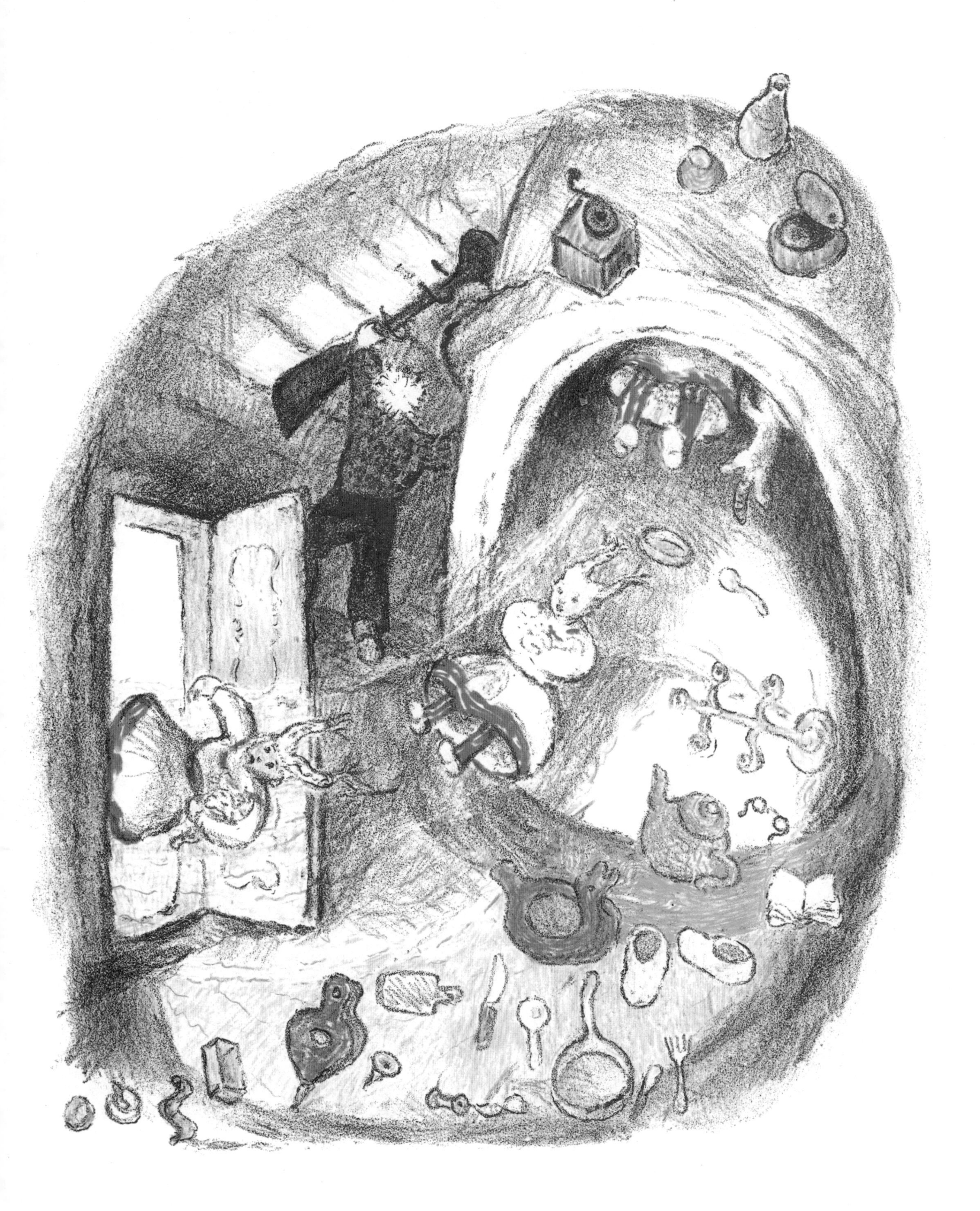

Lina, Sina, and Trina were lifted off their feet and blown straight up the chimney. Ola grabbed the blunderbuss and ran out the door,

just as Lina, Sina, and Trina came tumbling down the grass-thatched roof. They landed right in the arms of their mother. The bird was still perched on top of the storehouses.

Ola took aim and pressed the trigger. Off went the silver button. The blunderbuss thundered and roared and kicked so hard that everybody fell over backward.

When the smoke cleared away there were bright feathers floating all about. "What fine pillows these feathers will make," cried Lina, Sina, and Trina. "But where is the troll-bird?" asked Ola.

Then they spied it, way down at the bottom of the valley. It had plowed its way straight down the hill, tearing up the trees and leaving an open road behind it.

"How shall we ever get that big bird up to the farm so we can pluck it and roast it?" asked Ola.

"Blakken will pull and we will push," said Lina, Sina, and Trina. But for all they pushed and all they pulled, the troll-bird did not budge.

They got nine more horses from the farm. But the bird was so heavy that even ten strong horses couldn't move it.

So Lina, Sina, and Trina ran up to get the cows and the goats and the sheep. Even the pigs had to come.

At last, with all the animals hitched to the bird, they were able to drag it up to the farm.

The news went out that the terrible troll-bird was to end up on a roasting spit, and people came from far and wide to celebrate. They brought cakes and puddings and, yes, even a fiddler. Soon there was music and merrymaking all over the farm. Together they plucked

the troll rooster. From the down and feathers they made pillows and quilted puffs. From the claws they made pitchforks and from the beak a sturdy boat. From the tough skin they made twelve pairs of shoes, and the finest pair, of course, was for mother.

Then they hoisted the huge fowl up over a pit filled with glowing embers. Two strong horses pulled the ropes that turned the spit.

It was late at night before the bird was ready and the delicious smell of roast chicken filled the whole valley.

There was plenty of food to go around; one drumstick alone filled twelve hungry stomachs. The fiddler played his liveliest tunes and everybody sang with mouths full of meat.

Even the animals of the forest came, prancing and dancing on two legs. They too were glad to be rid of the evil troll-bird. It had been a menace to them all.

Little red-capped gnomes popped out from their secret hiding places in caves and behind boulders. And green-clad sprites, called hulder-maidens, came up from their world deep underground. They were enchantingly beautiful, and if it hadn't been for the cows'

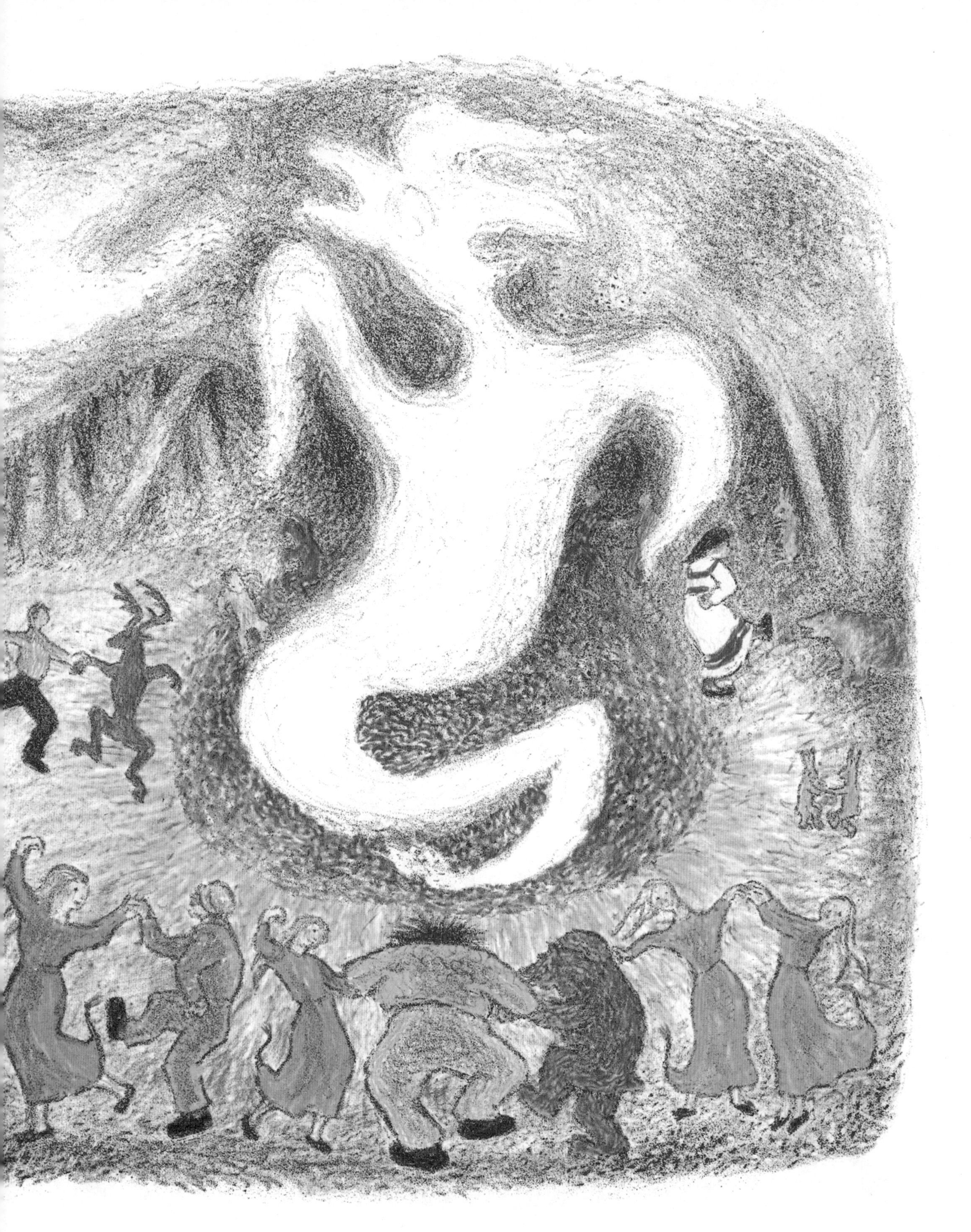

tails swishing behind them, they could have been taken for real girls. The hulder-maidens did not show themselves often, but on this night all creatures were friends. Joining hands and paws they danced merrily around the fire.

Toward daybreak the big mountain up the valley started to creak and groan. A stone door opened up and two moss-grown old trolls came out. They were Gygra and her husband, Jotun.

They often tramped about at night, looking for a pig, a bear, or a fat little boy to put into their stew-pot. Now they had come out to search for their rooster. They sniffed the air and Gygra growled, "Someone has roasted my rooster, my fine, fat fowl."

"Fo-fow-fowl," thundered echoes from all sides. Gygra was so angry that she almost burst.

"Don't burst," said Jotun. "We'll follow the smell and eat the roast ourselves." And with heavy steps they stomped down the valley, sniffing their way to the farm.

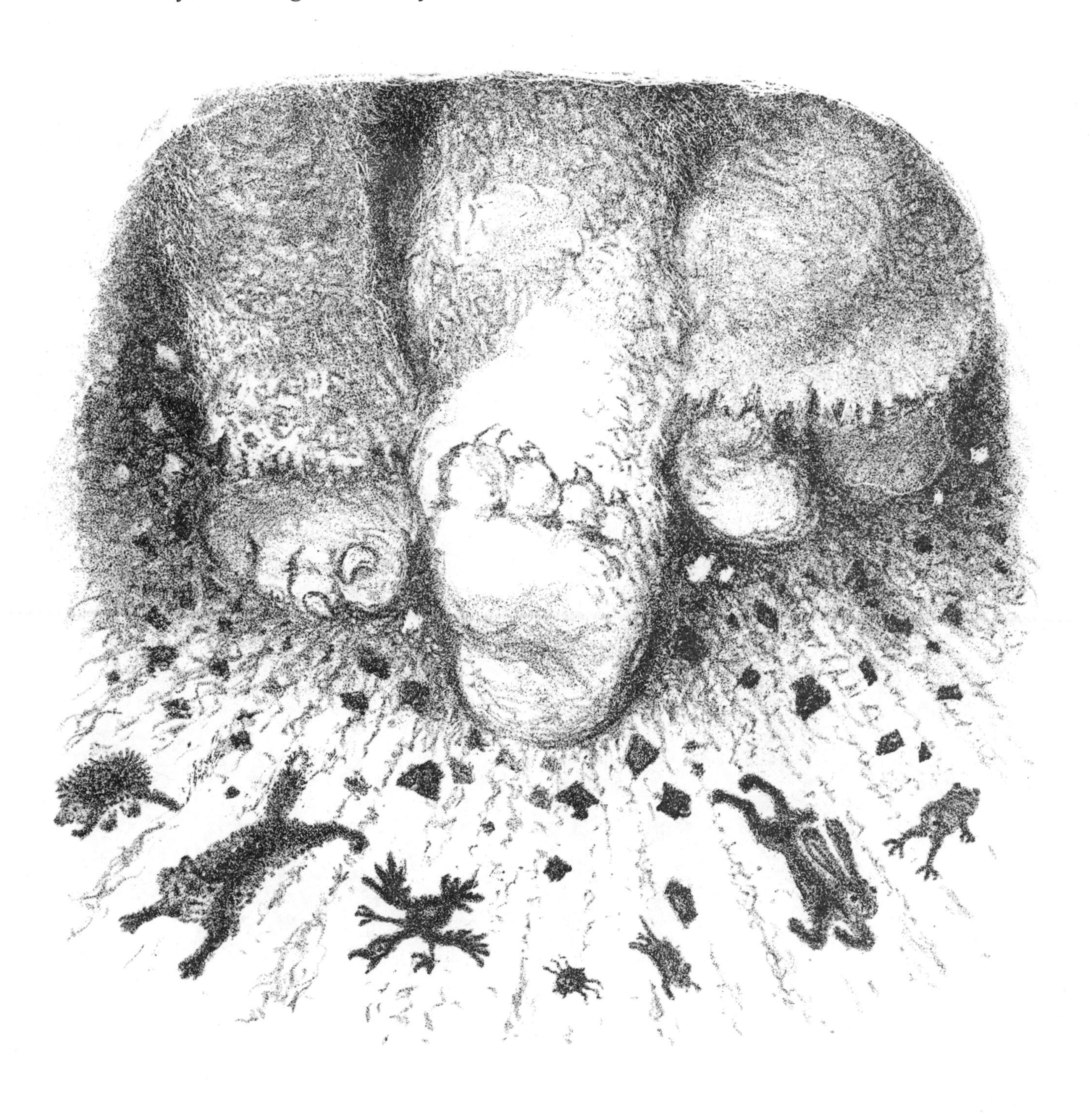

When the trolls reached the farm and saw that the bones of the bird had been picked clean, they flew into a rage.

"You have eaten our rooster," they roared. "For that we shall carry your houses into the mountain for little trolls to play with."

The fiddler dropped his fiddle, the gnomes rolled away like balls of gray yarn, the hulder-maidens vanished into the ground, the animals scattered into the woods, and the people ran into the houses and hid under beds, behind doors, and inside cupboards.

But not Ola and Lina, Sina, and Trina. They saw that the sun was about to rise, and they knew that trolls are creatures of darkness. Only when the sun is down can trolls walk about outside their mountain.

"Look," they cried. "Now see what will happen!" Just as the trolls reached for the houses, the sun peeped over the mountains.

As soon as the sun's rays hit them, the trolls turned to stone and burst with a bang. Moss-grown boulders and stones lay scattered all over the ground. Some looked like noses, some like ears, some

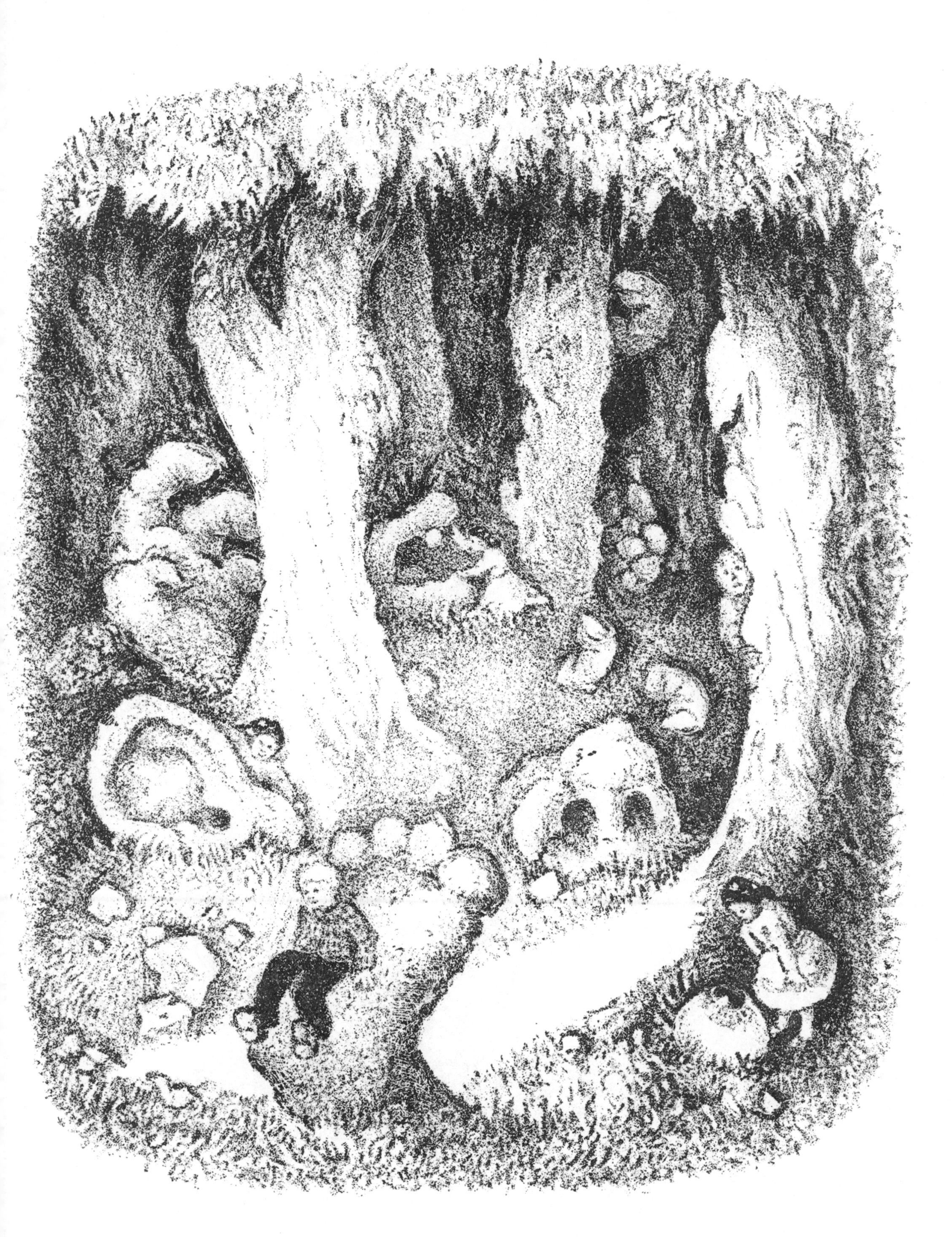

like fingers and toes. Now the people dared to come out from their hiding places. Shouting and laughing, they ran around looking at the strange new rocks.

Soon, tired from the long night, they went to the hayloft to sleep and snore. The pillows and quilts filled with troll-bird feathers were plump and soft.

But Ola, Lina, Sina, and Trina could not sleep. First they had to try the sturdy boat made from the troll-bird's beak.

Snip, snap, snout,

and now the tale is out.

INGRI MORTENSON and EDGAR PARIN D'AULAIRE met at art school in Munich in 1921. Edgar's father was a noted Italian portrait painter, his mother a Parisian. Ingri, the youngest of five children, traced her lineage back to the Viking kings.

The couple married in Norway, then moved to Paris. As Bohemian artists, they often talked about emigrating to America. "The enormous continent with all its possibilities and grandeur caught our imagination," Edgar later recalled.

A small payment from a bus accident provided the means. Edgar sailed alone to New York where he earned enough by illustrating books to buy passage for his wife. Once there, Ingri painted portraits and hosted modest dinner parties. The head librarian of the New York Public Library's juvenile department attended one of those. Why, she asked, didn't they create picture books for children?

The d'Aulaires published their first children's book in 1931. Next came three books steeped in the Scandinavian folklore of Ingri's childhood. Then the couple turned their talents to the history of their new country. The result was a series of beautifully illustrated books about American heroes, one of which, *Abraham Lincoln*, won the d'Aulaires the American Library Association's Caldecott Medal. Finally they turned to the realm of myths.

The d'Aulaires worked as a team on both art and text throughout their joint career. Originally, they used stone lithography for their illustrations. A single four-color illustration required four slabs of Bavarian limestone that weighed up to two hundred pounds apiece. The technique gave their illustrations an uncanny hand-drawn vibrancy. When, in the early 1960s, this process became too expensive, the d'Aulaires switched to acetate sheets which closely approximated the texture of lithographic stone.

In their nearly five-decade career, the d'Aulaires received high critical acclaim for their distinguished contributions to children's literature. They were working on a new book when Ingri died in 1980 at the age of seventy-five. Edgar continued working until he died in 1985 at the age of eighty-six.

TITLES IN THE NEW YORK REVIEW
CHILDREN'S COLLECTION

ESTHER AVERILL
Captains of the City Streets
The Hotel Cat
Jenny and the Cat Club
Jenny Goes to Sea
Jenny's Birthday Book
Jenny's Moonlight Adventure
The School for Cats

SHEILA BURNFORD
Bel Ria: Dog of War

DINO BUZZATI
The Bears' Famous Invasion of Sicily

INGRI AND EDGAR PARIN D'AULAIRE
D'Aulaires' Book of Animals
D'Aulaires' Book of Norse Myths
D'Aulaires' Book of Trolls
The Two Cars

EILÍS DILLON
The Island of Horses
The Lost Island

ELEANOR FARJEON
The Little Bookroom

RUMER GODDEN
An Episode of Sparrows

LUCRETIA P. HALE
The Peterkin Papers

MUNRO LEAF AND ROBERT LAWSON
Wee Gillis

NORMAN LINDSAY
The Magic Pudding

ERIC LINKLATER
The Wind on the Moon

E. NESBIT
The House of Arden

BARBARA SLEIGH
Carbonel: The King of the Cats

T. H. WHITE
Mistress Masham's Repose

REINER ZIMNIK
The Bear and the People
The Crane